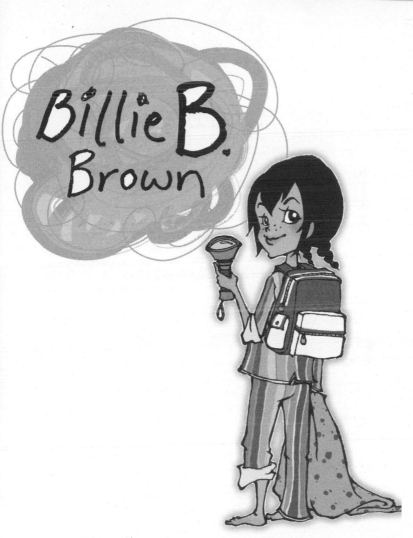

Billie B. Brown

www.BillieBBrownBooks.com

Billie B. Brown Books

The Bad Butterfly
The Soccer Star
The Midnight Feast

Hey Jack! Books

The Crazy Cousins
The Scary Solo
The Winning Goal

First American Edition 2012
Kane Miller, A Division of EDC Publishing

Text Copyright © 2010 Sally Rippin
Illustrations Copyright © 2010 Aki Fukuoka

First published in Australia in 2010 by Hardie Grant Egmont

For information contact:
Kane Miller, A Division of EDC Publishing
P.O. Box 470663
Tulsa, OK 74147-0663
www.kanemiller.com
www.edcpub.com

Library of Congress Control Number: 2011935695

Printed and bound in the United States of America
1 2 3 4 5 6 7 8 9 10
ISBN: 978-1-61067-097-5

The
Midnight
Feast

By Sally Rippin

Illustrated by Aki Fukuoka

Kane Miller
A DIVISION OF EDC PUBLISHING

Chapter One

Billie B. Brown has one blue flashlight, one big package of marshmallows and one brand-new tent. Do you want to know what the "B" in Billie B. Brown stands for?

Big.

Billie B. Brown says she is now big enough to go camping!

Do you know where Billie is going to go camping? In Jack's backyard.

Jack is Billie's best friend. He lives next door.

Brand-new tent

Blue flashlight

Big package of
marshmallows

Billie and Jack are going
to sleep in Billie's new
tent.

And guess what?

Billie and Jack are going to have a midnight feast! That's why Billie needs so many marshmallows.

Billie and Jack are sitting in the tent. They are planning their midnight feast. Jack has two bags of chips. Billie has some rice crackers and dip.

Jack's dad pokes his head into the tent flap. "Hey, kids, dinner's ready!"

"We don't need dinner," says Billie. "We've got heaps of food!"

"It's a long time until midnight," says Jack's dad. "And it's spaghetti bolognese!"

Jack looks at Billie.
"It's spaghetti bolognese," he says.

Spaghetti bolognese is
Billie's favorite.

"Um, OK," says Billie. "We'll just come in for dinner. But that's all!"

Billie and Jack run inside. They can smell the spaghetti. It makes their tummies **rumble**.

Billie and Jack eat two bowls of spaghetti each.

Then they run back
outside to their tent.
It is still light.

"Shall we have the
marshmallows now?"
Jack asks.

He reaches for the big
package full of pink and
white marshmallows.
They look delicious!

"No, silly!" says Billie. "They are for the midnight feast!"

"Oh," says Jack. "Maybe we can have the chips then?"

"OK then," says Billie. "And maybe the dip and rice crackers too. They can be our practice midnight feast."

"Good idea," says Jack.

Billie and Jack wriggle
with excitement.
Camping is so much fun!

Chapter Two

Billie and Jack get into their sleeping bags. They share a bag of chips. Then they eat the dip and rice crackers.

They will keep the marshmallows until midnight. But midnight feels like a very long way away. It's not even dark outside yet.

"Let's go and get a game!" Billie suggests. "I've got Uno at home."

"Cool!" says Jack.

So Billie and Jack unzip the tent and run out into Jack's backyard. They run along the fence until they get to the hole. Then they squeeze

through the hole into
Billie's backyard. Billie
and Jack run inside.
Billie's mom and dad are
watching TV in the
family room.

"Hi, kids!" Billie's mom
calls. "*Finding Nemo*'s on
tonight. It's starting in five
minutes."

"We're camping!" calls
Billie. "We can't watch TV
when we're camping!"

"But it's *Finding Nemo!*" says Jack to Billie.

Finding Nemo is Billie and Jack's favorite movie.

Billie frowns. "Oh, OK!" she says.

Billie and Jack sit down in the family room to watch.

Billie's dad makes them strawberries and ice cream and lets them eat in front of the TV.

"Teeth," says Billie's mom when the movie finishes.

"You don't brush your teeth when you go camping!" says Billie.

"Oh, yes, you do," says Billie's mom.

So Billie and Jack go to the bathroom to brush their teeth.

Jack keeps a spare toothbrush at Billie's house. Billie has one at Jack's house too.

When they have finished,

Billie and Jack peer out the back window. Now it is very dark outside.

"Are you sure you still want to sleep in the tent tonight?" Billie's mom asks.

"Of course!" says Billie. "We're camping!"

"Uh-oh!" says Jack. "I

left my flashlight inside
the tent."

"Me too," says Billie.
"How are
we going
to find our
way back in
the dark?"

"Don't worry," says
Billie's dad. "I'll take you

back. But I'm not going through the hole in the fence."

So Billie's dad takes them back over to Jack's house. But this time they go around the front way!

Chapter Three

Billie's dad tucks Billie and Jack into their sleeping bags. He gives them both a kiss.

"Are you sure you're OK out here?" Billie's dad asks.

"Of course!" says Billie. "We're big kids now!"

"Big people can still get scared," Billie's dad says.

"Well, not us!" says Jack.

If Jack's not scared, neither am I!

Billie's dad smiles
and zips up the tent.

Billie and Jack lie in their
sleeping bags. A little bit
of light shines onto the
tent from Jack's house,
but not much. Inside the
tent it is very dark.
And **very quiet**.

"What time is it?" Billie
asks Jack.

Jack turns on his flashlight and looks at his watch. "Nine-fifteen," he says.

"Hmm," says Billie. "It's still a long time until midnight."

Billie isn't sure if she
likes camping in the dark.
It was much more fun
during the day. But she
lies very quietly because
she doesn't want Jack to
think she is **scared**.

"Maybe we could just
have the feast now?"
Jack says.

"No, silly," says Billie.
"Then it won't be a
midnight feast.
That would be a nine-
fifteen feast!"

"Of course!" says Jack.
He switches off the
flashlight. Then he turns
it on again. "I'd better
leave the flashlight on,"
he says. "So we can tell

when it's midnight."

"Good idea," says Billie.

She wonders if Jack is
also a teensy bit scared of
the dark.

Billie and Jack snuggle
down into their sleeping
bags. They lie side by side
and listen to the sounds
of the night.

Suddenly Jack sits up.

"Did you hear that?"

he asks.

"What?" says Billie.

She sits up too.

Then she hears the noise.

It sounds like a low

growling.

"What's that?" says Jack.

"I don't know!" says Billie.

She feels **scared**. The growling sound gets louder. Billie and Jack hear a **scuffling** just outside the tent flap.

Then a dark shadow slides across the tent walls.

"A monster!" Billie and Jack scream together. "Mom! Dad!"

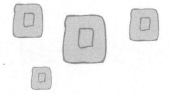

Chapter Four

Jack's dad pokes his head through the tent flap. "You kids OK?" he asks, smiling.

Billie and Jack are huddled together.

"We saw a huge monster!"
Jack says.

"It **growled** at us!"
Billie says.

"There's no such thing as monsters," says Jack's dad. "It was probably just a possum. Are you sure you kids don't want to come inside?"

Jack looks at Billie.

"I'm scared," he says

quietly.

"Me too!" says Billie.

She feels **glad** that Jack

feels the same as her.

"But I really wanted to

sleep in my new tent!"

"And have a midnight

feast!" Jack adds.

Billie is **disappointed**.
She wants so much to
sleep in the tent, but it is
too dark and scary outside.

Billie and Jack look
at each other. They are
trying to decide what
to do.

Then, Billie has a great
idea. A super-dooper idea!

Can you guess what
she's thinking?

Billie and Jack bundle
up their sleeping bags.
They pick up their trash
and the big package of
marshmallows.
Jack's dad helps them
pack up the tent. Then
they run across the
backyard to the warm
light of Jack's house.

Ten minutes later,
Billie and Jack are
in the tent again.
They are snuggled in
their sleeping bags, and
they are fast asleep.

Do you know where
Billie and Jack are
camping now?

On Jack's bedroom floor!

Oh dear! What about
their midnight feast?

It doesn't matter.
Billie and Jack can have
a midnight feast another
time. Maybe when they
are even bigger.

44